To Roy. Thank you for being a wonderful Pop Pop to LeAnna and Cameron.
JCB

To my dad, "Silly Grandpa"; my father-in-law, "Papa"; and Papa Joe
AGF

TIME FOR BED, OLD HOUSE

Janet Costa Bates

illustrated by AG Ford

CANDLEWICK PRESS

ISAAC LOVED THE NEW PAJAMAS he got for his first sleepover at Grandpop's house. He loved laughing and playing with Grandpop. But he didn't love the thought of sleeping away from home.

"I'm not sleepy," Isaac said.

"Then stay awake," Grandpop said. "But it's time to put the house to bed."

"I never heard of putting a house to bed," said Isaac.

"Well, little buddy," said Grandpop, "let me show you and Bear how it's done."

"First, you move kind of quiet and slow." Grandpop took soft, slow steps across the room. Isaac took soft, slow steps behind him. "Now let's make it nice and dark and cozy," Grandpop said, and he turned off the light.

Click. Click. Click.
"What's that noise?" asked Isaac.
He reached for Grandpop's hand.

"That's just Snuffles," Grandpop said. The old dog plodded across the floor, nails clicking. Isaac gave Snuffles a pat.

With Isaac and Snuffles following, Grandpop stepped softly down the hallway. He paused at the light switch and looked at Isaac. Isaac reached up and turned it off.

Squeak. Squeak. Squeak.
"What's that noise?" asked Isaac.

Grandpop brought Isaac over to the window and pointed. "The wind is blowing your swings back and forth," he said. Isaac could see them moving in the moonlight.

"Now, come on, sport. We're not done yet." Grandpop carefully pulled down the window shades. "Looks like the house is closing its eyes to sleep," he said.

Creak. Creak. Creak.
"What's that noise?" asked Isaac.

"This old house makes sleepy sounds, just like you," said Grandpop. "You yawn. You stretch. I bet you even snore."

"I don't think I snore," said Isaac.

Grandpop shrugged. "But if you're sleeping, how do you know?" He chuckled loudly, then caught himself and put his hand over his mouth.

"Come on, little pal," Grandpop said softly. They tiptoed up the stairs.

When Snuffles yawned a squeaky yawn, Grandpop put his finger to his lips and whispered, "Shhh, Snuffles. Shhh."

They went into Momma's old bedroom. "Time to read a bedtime story to the house," Grandpop said quietly to Isaac.

"But I can't read yet," Isaac said quietly to Grandpop.

"I bet you can read pictures." Grandpop settled himself into the big chair by the bed and held out a book to Isaac. "Just tell me what you see on each page."

Isaac climbed onto Grandpop's lap and described the first picture. "A little boy is looking out the window. There's snow on the ground." Isaac turned the page. "He's outside wearing a red jacket."

"Good job," said Grandpop. "Keep going."

When Isaac finished reading the pictures in the book, he rested his head on Grandpop's shoulder. He could hear him breathing slow and steady. He looked up and saw that he had read Grandpop to sleep.

Isaac carefully climbed off the chair.
He covered Grandpop with a blanket.

Then, taking soft, slow steps, Isaac
walked over to the window.

He gently closed the shade and
whispered, "Time for bed, old house."

When the grandfather clock chimed from the hallway,
Isaac put his finger to his lips. "Shhh, Mr. Clock. Shhh."

Isaac settled himself into bed, picked up a book,
and, in a soft voice, read the pictures to Bear.
When he was done, he quietly turned off the lamp.

Click. Click. Click.
He reached out to pet Snuffles.

Squeak. Squeak. Squeak.
He thought of the fun he and Bear
would have on the swings tomorrow.

Creak. Creak. Creak.
Tonight, he would sleep well in the old house.

And if that old house could hear, then it, too, would have heard bedtime noises.

DISCARD